HEX

'Exceptional . . . I'm still reeling from it, it is devastating . . . "the purest light attracts the most impenetrable darkness" – that line just resonates and resonates . . . a stunning book, thank you for this'
BBC RADIO SCOTLAND

'This series has already produced two works of note and distinction. It raises the question – if a country cannot re-tell its history, will it be stuck forever in aspic and condemned to be nothing more than a shortbread tin illustration? *Hex* and *Rizzio* are showing the way towards a reckoning, and about time too'
STUART KELLY, SCOTLAND ON SUNDAY

'*Hex*, for a book about such trauma and agony, is a crisp, clear book . . . elegant and angry in equal measure'
THE SCOTSMAN

'Unsurprisingly brilliant, a feminist war cry from one century to another as we spend the night with a young woman about to be slowly hanged as a witch. Beautiful, moving writing'
SARAH PINBOROUGH

'Small but mighty . . . the mere fact that this tale is based on real events gives the story a powerful, disturbing authenticity'
SCOTTISH FIELD

'*Hex* is stunning, so powerful . . . Beautiful work!'
SALENA GODDEN

'The magical and the realism are always in perfect balance . . . *Hex* is both a timely and timeless publication'
ALISTAIR BRAIDWOOD

HEX

Jenni Fagan

Polygon

First published in hardback in Great Britain in 2022 by Polygon,
an imprint of Birlinn Ltd. This paperback edition published
in Great Britain in 2022 by Polygon.

Birlinn Ltd
West Newington House
10 Newington Road
Edinburgh
EH9 1QS

www.polygonbooks.co.uk

2

ISBN 978 1 84697 622 3
EBOOK ISBN 978 1 78885 483 2

Typeset by 3btype, Edinburgh
Printed and bound in Great Britain by Clays Ltd, Elcograf S.p.A.

For Geillis Duncan

1

Iris

Midnight

Open invitation sent (via seance):

1st August 2021 — to cell on High Street, 4th December 1591

Elements: Null + Air

I was out in the Null. In perpetuity, it seemed, I was bodiless and formless until things began to appear. A row of oil-lit street-lamps. A cobbled road sloping down. The moon a thin smile. City trees bending their boughs so far back! The winds, wild! Tall tenement buildings line the road to Castlehill.

A witch will die here in the morning.

I descend a full three levels below the city of Edinburgh into a low-arched stone corridor. A guard is nestled in a nook. He peers into the gloom. I need him to go, so I can come to you. Coalesce right next to his ear — whisper.

— Back out you go, into the Null, go on, your body is so heavy isn't it?

— Who is that?

I don't know how I know how to do this, but I do. I always have. I gently help his consciousness to separate from his body.

— It's only dreaming . . .

I say it into his ear, low and over and over, until his eyes close and his head lolls. To be able to do something like this you must learn not to have those around you drink your energy. I have learnt the hard way. As a child I used to give away light like it was nothing. Those without it would fill themselves up with all that good energy like I was an eternal font. The purest light attracts the most impenetrable darkness. Great giant moths-of-death come flying for it at night. All across the world. They will smother any source until all they have left is an empty husk. I will pay a price for this. That is how it goes.

With shaking hands that don't feel quite solid at all, I take off his boots, retch. (Can a spirit-dweller vomit? Yes, yes, yes, when a stench is this bad they can.) He has horned yellow toenails, thick and fungal. Throw his boots away down a tiny wee well. If he wakes he won't get anywhere quickly. You need time to prepare, Geillis Duncan. They will execute you in the morning.

Strike a match!
We have so little time.
I must hurry now.

2

Iris

12.37 a.m.

Open invitation pursued (via astral travel):
1st August 2021 — to cell on High Street, 4th December 1591
Elements: Null + Air

Your cell is several floors below the city. It is far below footfall, or taverns, or flats; below beds, or kitchens, or hugs, or hope, or church, or prayer, or freedom, or laughter, or air; below shuttered windows, or dogs asleep in front of fires. It is so far below the seasons they might as well not exist. There is only one kind of weather in here — freezing cold and cloaked in darkness. The air is stagnant. I must wait a minute. Make sure the guard does not wake. The last thing I could take is him coming to you. You are down here somewhere, Geillis Duncan. I'm willing to go as far as I have to — so you are not alone on this, the last night of your life. I put a call out — to the ether — for you.

I have never channelled directly like this before, was far too afraid to do so.

Travelled time all my life.

Have had spirits come to me, go through me, had them drag me out of my body and throw me across rooms or ceilings all night long. I have seen one half-naked, just out the bath, holding a big knife. I heard them and hosted them before I knew how to form words, or smile. For you, though, I have been out in the Null. I was waiting. Unsure what this will mean for my health or my life. Will I get to go back? Five hundred years between us, Geillis Duncan — it's such a little leap really.

A conversation between two witches across time.

I am nervous.

I miss you.

Don't ask me why I feel like this because I don't know.

Some people might think it is not possible to so desperately miss someone you do not yet know, or a home you have never had, but I do. I have done so my whole life. I miss people I have never met. Mourn them. Even more than those who have already, one by one, been taken from me.

The hangman will be here by dawn.

I reach for the guard's keys.

He has put a padlock through them, and they are locked

into a metal hoop high up on the wall. There are no risks
taken with witches. If only! The hangman might have
found your cell door ajar. Dust spiralling through a wan
sliver of light. On the floor, a single feather. His boots
would pivot in the dirt. Pound back up the corridor. Onto
the Close, up onto the High Street where people would
already be walking by with their scrubbed morning faces,
clean and ready – to watch Geillis Duncan die.

   – She took flight!

   – What?

   – The prisoner, the witch, she is gone!

   – Where?

   – The Devil took her, or a familiar. The last guard is in
a spellbound stupor, the man is barely there!

   – Idiot . . .

I'd love to hear the roar. Who would dare stop a good
hanging? All the women I know would. Any one of us!
We'd each come back and do this gladly. The murder of
Geillis Duncan is to be performed for the State and the
King and the bailiff who accused her; it is for the
God-fearing, it is for ordinary people who like a good
hanging. For those who need to hate. To elevate themselves
on hatred. If you were not hanged in the morning, Geillis,
how many people would go home feeling cheated?
Disappointed not to see you die in front of them? They
want to be able to say they were there when Geillis
Duncan died. To dine out on the story for years. There was

a witch we saw killed! I turn down the last tiny winding corridor — you have to be at the end somewhere along here. Your murder is a message for the masses. King James's enemies will shudder. Will his wife? Anne: fourteen and wed to a man who likes men and is paranoid he'll be caught out for it. Over three hundred tailors worked on Anne's wedding dress. It is all spectacle. Weddings, births, hangings. There is a bloodlust in humans. Let's watch a girl hang to death! The King is showing all his might! Who would fight a man who has taken down the Devil himself? King James didn't start this particular witch-hunt, but he will certainly finish it. How does he fight the Devil?

Well, now you ask!

Via teenage girls!

Doesn't everyone?

We go after the Devil via womb-bearers — they are weak for him!

Widows!

Did she inherit?

A woman?

On her own?

Is she tall?

Is she ugly?

Does she twitch?

Is she too smart?

Did she look a man right in the eye?

Did she heal a pig?

Did she birth a child who died?

Did she speak — harshly?

No!

They won't tolerate that.

A woman's voice is a hex. She must learn to exalt men always. If she doesn't do that, then she is a threat. A demon whore, a witch — so says everyone and the law. So say the King and his guards. So say the witch-pricker and his sadistic friends. So say the husbands, the haters, the wives, the daughters, the God-fearing — demons are always trying to kill them, so they know. So says the hangman who sleeps with Bible in hand.

There is your cell, Geillis Duncan! Finally. It has taken so long to get here that I must not cry. I throw my arms up. A billow of dust falls — I have finally coalesced, into a slightly more solid form. Your cell is tiny and dark. You are still a child, really.

— Who's that there?

— Can you see me, Geillis?

— Sssh. If he hears you, it'll be me that gets it. I can't see you properly — it's too dim. What are you? Are you a demon?

— My name is Iris.

— Are you mad? Iris, do you know what they'll do if they find you here? How did you get in?

— I travelled through time.

— Liar.

— I did, to get to you.

— Why?

— So you wouldn't be on your own on this of all nights.

You shuffle forward a touch, less scared than a minute ago.

— Are you my familiar?

— No.

Almost up at the cell bars, you look right at me.

— Are you sure?

Rats scrape in the corner.

You hold my gaze.

Head turned away, eyes towards me — the outline of your nose and forehead and chin is marked in moonlight; you look like a silver face on a ten-pence coin.

— No, I don't think that's possible, Geillis. I mean, I didn't think . . .

— Of that?

— No.

— I see. How will you get back exactly, Iris from the ether?

— I don't know.

You smile then, a small giggle. You have an indent in your chin, soft hairs at your temple; your skin is so thin it seems precarious that it holds your blood and bones and organs and heart and soul.

— You are thinking of my insides, my dear strange visitor?

— No.

— Liar.

— So!

— You know any minute now all my innards may spill onto the floor — at your feet. You'll sit in my sticky blood, my heart will still beat next to my liver and kidneys, and my eyes will rotate in a crimson pool, staring at you, my mouth too — open and laughing!

— Geillis . . .

— What? You thought I'd play nice? Tell me what tonight's guard looks like? I need to know if he is the one who visits my cell before morning. I don't think I can take it if it is him, not even one last time.

Your fist is balled tight.

Jaw set like marble.

Eyes hooded in darkness, and you are full of a fear so pure it smells like rotting pears.

— The guard won't get back up again tonight, I promise.

— You did that for me?

— I tried, Geillis. You know what you said about a familiar? I was the one — I called out to you, but did you . . . ?

— I don't know, Iris, did I?

Our thoughts march like mechanical clocks.

— The hangman will be here early.

— I know.

You open your hands like a prayer book. Ankles so thin. Skirt bunched up and dirty. Your right leg sticks out from your skirt at an angle like they broke it and didn't let it set right afterwards. You are all bone. More than pallid! You are a girl made of moon. Dark eyes that might have been some other colour once, but they took the pigment out of them and you are already – gone.

3

Iris

1.29 a.m.
Seance (a final supper):
1st August 2021 — cell on High Street, 4th December 1591
Elements: Null + Air

The ether is a tributary going out across the universe, and we can travel it in any direction — human souls don't live in bodies for so long. We are more magic than flesh. I am linked by atoms to you, Geillis Duncan. By blood too! In the dirt in front of your cell door there is an imprint of two knees. I can feel your breath on my skin. I'd give you all my light. We started in the Null, you and I. Bodiless. Some of us still remember this, some (like us) never forget.

— They took your shine, Geillis.

— Excised it.

— It's not hard to separate soul from body and leave just a shell for those who know how.

— Aye, that is true. Iris, do you know what I hate?

— I can guess.

— I hate that this cell smells of rusty buckets corroding with piss.

— Think of a better place.

You lean on the bars and look at me.

— My grandmother's house smelled of lavender. Sunlight came through her kitchen window each afternoon, and it would land on her armchair, and I would sleep there curled up warm as a cat when I was a child.

I hold out my hand so whatever heat I have may warm you.

The next bit will be harder.

There's a coiled rope.

It's next to the hangman's bed. Waiting to bite into the soft pale flesh of your neck. The hangman is asleep in a tavern. Early morning he will rise, breakfast. Look at you, Geillis, with a touch of laughter still to your eyes as you inspect me, your fists tiny, your arms bruised, your knuckles white and covered in scrapes, your hair fallen out in clumps, your heart hammering manically – like a bird's.

— Can you stop them, Iris?

— No.

— So what can you do?

You are angry then and rightly so – we both resent the relentless approach of morning.

– Here's a blanket. Put it around your shoulders. Do it for me.

– How are you doing this, Iris?

– Never mind that – warm yourself, please, Geillis, you need warmth . . .

– What, for the last time?

– Aye. The last one – you shouldn't be cold tonight.

You pull the blanket around you and sink into it. It is as soft as I could summon, a deep mustard colour and made of pure wool.

– You just have to do one more thing for me, Geillis: pull that crate over in front of you. That's it. This might take a wee minute, so be patient and don't worry – it's no trick, it's no spell, I have nothing to do with devils or demons. Neither, my beautiful girl, have you – not now, not ever; we don't have to buy into the fears of men, even if they kill us for them.

– I like you, Iris.

– Thanks. I like you too, Geillis.

1. Close eyes.

2. Picture polished cutlery until it appears – a silver fork, sharp-toothed, a bone-handled knife.

– What are you doing?

Your eyes are round and tear-filled.

3. Focus harder!

– Sssh sssh, Geillis.

4. A bowl fills itself with thick hot meaty broth just like how your grandmother used to make it.

– Iris!

You clap your hands.

5. Make sure there is a pinch of sea salt, a touch of pepper, thick-cut bread with butter, cheese (three kinds of Cheddar), all in pretty bowls. The spirit feels like it will become trapped in this cell for eternity. To cure fear, you must treat them like a queen.

– I am thirsty, Iris . . .

6. A small bottle of spirits.

– Pudding?

– Aye.

7. A large clay bowl filled with hot rhubarb crumble, huge dollops of clotted cream. And on a jutting-out crag of stone on the cell wall, place two candles – long enough to burn all night.

– Is this real?

– Try . . .

The spoon clatters, then you slow down visibly to savour the broth's warmth. I don't care if I sleep for a year after this, it is the least I can do. Your hands flutter across the makeshift table.

Aye, there is a weapon.

– We shouldn't look at that; it is . . . is it consciousness, Iris?

It is, and it has a luminescence. It sparkles like phosphorescence. I let you eat in private. Close my eyes. You don't need an audience for this most intimate of acts. To feed yourself. To raise your hand. To eat slowly so your stomach can take more. I want to comb your hair and wash your face gently in soapy water. I want to clean and mend your clothes, make up a warm bed for you. I want to kill all your enemies, then cradle you like a child. I want to sing lullabies to you all night. The food and bowl disappear.

You sit with a flush to your cheeks that wasn't there before.

— Do you want me to tell you stories, Geillis?

— Isn't that the only way to get through this kind of a night?

— If I could open this cell door! I'd take your hand, tiptoe down the corridor with you, then up onto the Close. We'd run in silence together through Edinburgh — the back streets, as I did as a girl — and the moon would (for one night) keep lookout for us. We would find someone in a tavern or at the docks who could take you far, far away from here, where the King and his men would never find you, so you could begin anew.

— It's too late for that, Iris.

You hiss the words so quietly they appear to have been spoken by the air itself. Air talks to Null. Null coalesces into voice. I glance behind me. I watch the guard's chest rise and fall. He can't die, not tonight, or they'll do worse to you in the morning.

4

Geillis Duncan

3 a.m.

The argument (a visitation can be real):
1st August 2021 — cell on the High St, 4th December 1591
Elements: Null + Air

I walk slowly up and down inspecting my pretty visitation. I go over the same route I've followed in this cell over and over as if it were the sandy paths near North Berwick beach, with tufts of bleached grass and daisies and the smell of the sea. In all hours of the day I have tried to take myself there whilst on long walks in a dark, damp, stone cell. Dust tickles the back of my throat. It is always up my nose. There is dirt in my scalp, on my skin. I walk from furthest corner to furthest corner. Nothing can hide that way. If anyone comes in, they do so via the cell door. I see them coming. It is important not to let anyone come up behind you. This though, this . . . sweet, tired-looking Iris. I don't know what she is. I don't know how she got here. I have my own ideas about it, though. It was me, maybe. I brought her here. I rub my hands together for warmth. They are chapped and dry, and the skin is red and flaky. I ignore my sore feet and continue to pace. I should try to ask her more, just to be sure.

— Are you a demon?

— It depends, Geillis.

— On what?

— Who you ask!

We both laugh until a mistrusting gloom pulls over me like a shadow across the moon. I am not who I was before. Those men did what they did. Their presence is still on my skin. They brought a cold darkness. It has become a part of me. They took my warmth. Gave me all the sorrow I could carry. They told lies so I would be left in here to die and they would never have to look at me again.

— Were you sent by the Devil to trick me, Iris?

— No! My grandmother told me when I was a little girl that you and I are related by blood — although it wasn't by marriage, I know that much.

— How's that?

— We're not the marrying kind, Geillis.

— Sensible.

— Necessary.

— How did you hear about me, then?

— They write about you in books.

— They do?

— Are you smiling at me, Geillis Duncan? On this — the last day of your life?

— Just for a second . . .

We grin at each other like idiots.

— What do you women do in hundreds of years from now then, Iris from the ether?

— We look over our shoulder far too often.

— Aye.

You laugh wryly.

— We try to look bigger than we are sometimes. At other times we have to be smaller than we are. We do other things. Try to take down governments. Make great art. Keep others. Work without anyone noticing what we do for whole lifetimes sometimes. We hold hands. Drink too much or not at all. We traverse boundaries whilst looking ordinary. We give beauty and patience and science and our talent and our hearts and what was once firm in our bodies — we bestow our lives to this world, most often unseen.

You nod like a wise sage. The healer in you is taking the measure of me. We are nose to nose now. Even in the dim I can see a faint hint of freckles. I picture you young and strong, pelting your way across a beach, laughing like I used to do.

— Go on, Iris.

– We take our chances if we go out after darkness. We often walk down the middle of the road at night.

– Same.

– We know that every close or alley or road might appear like it has an exit, but it may in fact be one without end.

– Aye.

– If the State wanted us less dead, they'd do more about our murders.

– They don't?

– It depends.

– On what?

– How much money your family has, or the colour of your skin, those make up an unfathomable number of ignored murders. It might depend on what day it is, if there is a big news story elsewhere, or there are no gratuitous details for people to read over their morning coffee, then it probably still won't capture the news.

– Does the King order them?

– In some places, I suppose but no it's mostly just men doing what they feel entitled to do, certain women's deaths seem like they are almost, well, expected. In really poor neighbourhoods, or in areas of prostitution, you'd think that those women's murders appear acceptable, even, to some, and they are certainly far less questioned than others. There are those that hunt women or children who nobody cares about.

— Why?

— Because many of those crimes will see a total lack of consequence — no justice for their victims' families.

— There was a group of men, Iris, around my bed.

— I know.

— David Seaton made them shave me from head to toe, bald as they could.

— It's horrific.

— They wrapped a rope around my head, wound it tighter and tighter to crush my skull.

— I hate them.

— I felt my own bones crunch. Blood leaked out my ears. They held my legs open wide. Rammed things inside me. Metal, sticks, wood, a poker from the fire — until I bled and was raw. They turned me over, Iris . . . everything inside my body felt like it was burning, like I was on fire, like I was already in hell and they were the demons surrounding me, and it is for their crimes I will die!

— You are right.

— There were ten of them in there at one point. Grown men! Husbands, merchants; some had been friends since they were kids. The world kept turning black. They'd use salts to bring me back. They brought out the pilliwinks. Screwed bolts tight enough on my fingertips that all my nails split. I begged. I screamed. Why would they do that, Iris? They weren't human at that point. Nothing I recognise as human, anyway. They were worse than beasts, worse than devils, frenzied, caught so far up in it I thought they'd kill me there and then, and I prayed for release. They kept me just alive enough – to find even more ways to hurt me.

– Drink some water, Geillis, breathe.

– I screamed! People just walked by David Seaton's house the whole time. Nobody knocked on that door to help me. I begged, pleaded, said I'd do or say literally anything, but they liked what they were doing – far too much – so they just kept going.

– I hope they all die horribly.

– I do too.

– He was desperate to accuse someone, torture them enough so they'd accuse Euphame of being a witch for him, so he could try and get her money, and there I was right under his feet sweeping the grate.

– What reason did he use to accuse you?

– I helped women birth, I helped calves, I knew how to pick the right herbs to cure a headache, and I had a terrible want in me to go out at night and see the stars.

– Do you know, Geillis, I like to think about what would happen if the women of now went out to march for the women of then. And if . . . the women of then marched with the women of now.

– I would do that, Iris, we all would.

– Would you?

– Aye, all the witches in the faraway world you come from and here too, all together, marching.

— They say there is no such thing as witches, but that doesn't account for alchemy or instinct. We bring life from our bodies where before there was nothing. Null — absence, then life. What a thing!

— You must think I am a dream too, Iris.

— No, Geillis, you feel as real as anything else to me. I wish a particular kind of hell for those who put you here. The thing is, men don't know why they are here. None of us do. Not really. Tall stories only make tall churches. Not reality.

— No?

— Men want to know how they got trapped on earth. Don't they? It's an issue. What does each one of them see when he turns around to work it out? He sees a woman. Every single one of them sees the exact same thing. There is no man on this earth who didn't get here except by a woman parting her thighs! We are portals. Humans emerge from our bodies into a world without explanation. Some men hold a brutal kind of grudge for that. They hold hatred in their heart. They fear us — for bringing them out of the Null and into this. They want to kill us because we create their lives from our bodies. What kind of alchemy is that? What kind of a power? Within our flesh, we make flesh. Whilst we are reading books, working, fighting, sitting on the bus, we form atria, blood, lungs, legs, nails, hair, eyes, ears. Not all make it. We try again, or we don't. We bear pain. We bear loss. We serve a customer coffee when we are feeling anxious and achy and dead tired on our feet, but we still offer a smile, and right at that moment inside us – unseen – is that first stretch and yawn in amniotic fluid. At some point we cross ourselves and summon to each being a human soul. They say there is no such thing as magic! Tssssssk! So existence is explainable by – what? Devils and gods? Don't make me spit on all the textbooks.

– Iris?

– What?

– I would like to say I have no clue what you are talking about, but I do. I also know what heresy and blasphemy sound like, and if they heard what came out your mouth they'd hang you before they hang me.

– True.

– Be quiet now, my strange wee familiar! I need to sleep.

I curl up in the corner of my cell with my head on my arm. It will go numb, but there will be some warmth between me and the stone. Bunch my skirts all under me. She pushes the blanket toward me and I take it, forgetting it was still there. As I begin to drift away, watched over by Iris, I think of Anne, the child-queen. So much fuss made on her behalf because she is a girl married to a king – they cannot go far enough to bring her material and influence. She sleeps on the finest bed sheets in the palace whilst I am here, waiting for the hangman's footsteps.

5

Iris

3.44 a.m.
Testimony (bearing witness):
1st August 2021 – cell on High St, 4th December 1591
Elements: Null + Air

We have played noughts and crosses in the dust on the floor. You drew the hangman's gallows. I dusted over it with my hands. You did a drawing of the beach at North Berwick, which is the place you have told me you miss most, other than your grandmother's kitchen. We both drew cauldrons sailing out on the bay. Hundreds of them! Then we laughed. I wish there were such a thing for all the witches to sail out in. All the women! All the girls, all the boys and the good men too – maybe there could be giant soup-pots for the big ones. I am so thirsty now. It feels like I'm made of dust. Perhaps I am. This thirst won't be sated until I return to some other form. Somewhere out there is a different time, although it is less likely each minute that I will return to it.

– Is it right that a witch-pricker is paid by the hour?

– Aye, Iris. That wasn't how Seaton was going to pay off his debt, though. I didn't know Euphame. She was married to Seaton's wife's brother. He made me accuse her, because he wanted his wife to try to get her brother and Euphame's inherited money. I'm the reason an innocent women was burned to death at the stake.

You try hard to swallow, blink tears back.

– Now they say David Seaton swaggers around town like he beat the Devil himself. Hasn't paid for a drink once since – the King gave him gold and everything. Seaton took me to the King with my fingers mangled by pilliwinks, they forced me to play the Jew's harp for him, the way they said I had played it for the Devil.

– You're the first person on record to play the Jew's harp.

– Am I?

– Aye.

You look happy for a second, and lines and darkness lift, and I see a glimpse of your face before all this. You don't need to know this because soon you will die, but you can tell without me saying that I too have had men walk into a room. I too was a child. We say girl. We say woman.

We say things. They claimed you could bring winds to the North Sea. Of course you could! That cold wind kissed your forehead long before the Devil was rumoured to do so. I have stood on the shores at North Berwick. Hundreds of years after you! I'd say your name. Raise my arms. Bring a storm down gladly. Black-tipped waves to batter off rocks. Utter euphoria! If I get back through the ether, one day I'll swim in those waves, and I will think of you there, Geillis Duncan. Jumping each wave and laughing, a girl with nobody's eyes upon you unless they held love.

— They kept saying we had all gone out onto the bay in cauldrons.

— They said there were hundreds of you?

— Aye. They said we brought a storm to stop the King and his bride coming to land. They said we were out there with the Devil plotting against both of them. I lied in the end. I said I'd been in a boat called *The Grace of God* – not a cauldron – with the Devil and a coven. I said we drank wine. Sailed out on the Firth of Forth for days, singing, dancing! There had been a storm, see. There was a ship bringing gifts for the King and his new queen. It left from Burntisland, and forty people drowned before it reached Leith. Then later, when he tried to get Anne here, there was another storm. Agnes Sampson said we'd been trying to 'stay the Queen' from arriving safely to her husband in Scotland.

— Stay the Queen?

– Aye, stop her from coming in.

– They said Agnes had known what the King and Queen had said in private on their honeymoon, didn't they?

– Aye, Iris, that was the proof the King needed. Had to kill us then.

– And then Agnes got pregnant?

– She did, aye – that baby was born to stop a king from killing a witch.

– What a way to arrive in the world.

– Isn't it?

– Didn't stop them killing her after, though.

– No, it didn't.

– And the King said you were all creating the storms – you, Euphame, Barbara, Agnes, John?

– Yes, that we were all in cauldrons across that bay bringing storms to stop his wife from arriving, and to try and kill the King himself.

– It's not like the North Sea doesn't get bloody stormy anyway in Scotland!

You throw back your head and laugh loudly. I glance behind me. There is no movement from the guard.

– That's a point, Iris, I didn't mention it in the trial. Would have been cheeky, aye: It was the weather, your honour! It's bloody Scotland! Don't kill me for that. They also said I went to North Berwick church at All Hallows' Eve and led a procession by playing tunes on my Jew's harp.

I only admitted to using magic once, though. No matter how much they tortured me. I said I cast a spell on a hat belonging to a laird. I thought if I confessed to something small they might stop hurting me. There were also the cats. They said we were casting them into the sea in Leith, that we put spells on them – this was how they said we mostly brought the storms, not just with the cauldrons. And then they'd been saying Euphame MacCalzean had been at the *maleficia* thing for years – they said she'd killed her husband by magic, and that's treason, punishable by burning to death, then they said she'd done away with her wee nephew as well – just a young boy he was too. Then there was her thing with the Earl of Bothwell, which everyone knew about, and Bothwell hates the King with a vengeance.

– It all makes horrible sense.

– It does, in a way. King James has fear too, because they chopped his mother's head off, and all through his childhood attempts were made on his life, and he'd lie with any boy before a woman – but if I said that before the hangman's rope, who would hear me anyway? They have my testimony. I can't take it back!

– Aye, you can.

– It won't stop them killing me, Iris.

– No, but you can still say it if you want to. You have the right to tell the truth, and what can they take from you now anyway?

– I never thought of that.

My heart!

Your hand up to touch mine, lightly.

– I'd have said anything they wanted me to say in the end, Iris. I said that Napier and MacCalzean were witches – and the others, I said we'd been with the Devil and with other men and women all at once. He was insistent upon that, Seaton – that was the story he kept making me say over and over to him and his vile son and their pals, a neighbour's husband too. Ten men in that room, but they said there were five. For the worst bit two had to leave. I could hear them being sick in the back garden because of what the others were doing to me.

Your face is right before mine, and then . . . it is gone.

It's as if my eyes are closed.

We float.

All around us is space and darkness; bodiless – we will drift again awhile.

Trying too hard to stay together only makes this faint link go further away. All states of seance must be held so lightly.

6

Iris

4 a.m.

I know her more now (my friend):
1st August 2021 — cell on High St, 4th December 1591
Elements: Null + Air

O ut here we are safe. They can't get us. We can fight in element what we can't in flesh. We have to fly. Leave this mortal coil as often as we can. It has too many wrongs for us. The things they say! Our power must be homage to a man, even if he is the Devil, no? We must take what talent is in us naturally and bend at the feet of a male angel (fallen and evil), our only want to do his bidding, to kiss his rancid arse. Our tongues (especially) must not be our own.

To curse.

To use words.

To have them hang on the air . . .

Who would listen to the tongue of one who has kissed the Devil's arse?

How can women be truth-tellers when we brought down the Garden of Eden and are weak for such deceit and evil?

It's so . . . neat.

Bring upon a woman only shame. Make sure there is nothing she can say that could be taken as truth! Take the only thing she owns – her voice, her mind. Take it. Grind it into something pestilent. Line her up as dust and imbibe. What a way to get high! Absorb her. Destroy what brought you here. Power is not something women are allowed to own easily or – often – at all, let alone learn to wield.

Not by law!

The church says no.

Education does not teach what should be taught.

Girls learn to shine in secret.

We learn there are many reasons not to draw the eyes of men towards us; and if we do, there can be no gain in it. We dip our head first. We are meant to not raise our gaze, and that has been bored into us for centuries. We are meant to never let a look appear too direct. Don't be confrontational. Play nice – so nobody kills you. That won't always work, though. Be careful of men's motives. Hunch your shoulders! It is a great misfortune for a girl to be tall. To so easily look anyone in the eye. Or worse, look down on them. Hunch! Put those heels away. That click, click, click, click is Morse code for rapists. It says their sentences will be lenient or non-existent. If only she didn't wear stilettos. If only she didn't walk through a park. If only she didn't go out at night. If only those smart, brilliant sisters had realised police officers would later take selfies by their dead bodies. That the papers would sell it as part of the story. As if any human is a story. Not someone who means everything in the entire world to another human. Who is the reason they get up and work and fight and love. Almost nothing was said about the policemen who did that – why? In that case it was because those women had brown skin. What's to say? What's your point? Those officers are men with families. What is the message to all men who want to kill? Pick your corpses wisely. Maybe there will be just a little rap on the knuckle or a public joke at the dead's expense. You tell me what message goes out to every man, woman, boy and girl? What is it? Spell it out. They said you brought the wind to you, Geillis Duncan. Of course you did. There's not a storm on this earth didn't come from a woman – it's what happens when they clip our souls! I am grateful for the men and women who told me to bow my head to nobody.

That my voice was only mine to own.

I am here because of them.

Can feel coolness around me, and I'm sad to leave the Null this time.

— Are you still here, Geillis?

— I keep having fevery dreams, Iris.

You shake your head, run a dry tongue across cracked lips. You are hunched over like a wee stone gargoyle with a bitter wee face.

— What did you see?

— I saw the face of Agnes Sampson, and she said it was all my fault.

— Guilt is the shape of rats!

— They'll eat me.

— I'll shush them away.

— Keep one eye on the guard, please, Iris. I'm scared he'll come in here one last time.

— If he does, I'll kill him.

— How?

— I'll sing to him. I've got the voice of a siren — it's not a voice to launch a thousand ships, it's a voice to sink them.

— Was it you who started that storm then, Iris?

— Aye, might have been.

— You are funny!

— You know what really brings the storms, Geillis?

— What?

— A storm arrives at the exact second when a girl learns she'll never be free.

— Aye.

— When hope dies, it brings hail.

– It's the grandmothers and witches who walked before us send lightening, Iris, ay?

– Aye, they send blizzards to let us know they're still near. A sandstorm drifts across the desert. Dust devils. Whirlwinds! Grey thunderclouds rumble out for hundreds of miles across still plains – all animals, birds and insects instinctively retreat. A black shelf cloud presses down upon a lake, one man in a boat looks up towards it; or a tornado throws up that first twist of air to spiral – like a grey rose of destruction set to annihilate all in her wake. There is not a storm on earth has not come from a woman. The earth and skies and stars and galaxies and light and dark itself are all our mother. It is she who birthed us.

Girls learn to hide themselves, and boys, they do too. Boys too.

– Iris?

– Aye?

– I'm so cold.

– Put your head under your dress, Geillis – see, like this – pull the neck up over your head and breathe inside the material so the heat of your breath is not wasted. It will help keep you warm.

– How do you know that?

– I used to do it when I had nowhere to stay.

– I'm dizzy, Iris.

– It's fear.

– They are going to hang me.

– I know.

– I can't breathe!

– You can! Geillis, you are panicking. Listen, focus on my voice. I'll tell you stories, and you can just drift away – you don't need a broomstick to visit other places, our kind never did. A born witch needs no wand, or pentagram, or herb, or broomstick – those are props for those who like ceremony, or for those who don't have the imagination to use magic without them. You and I, we don't need any contraptions to fly.

– Iris?

– Aye?

– Will you hold my hand?

Just like that we are solidly formed together out of air.

You put your hand out – palm up. Mine is bigger and warmer: I press what strength I have into you.

– I can only see your outline. What do you look like, Iris?

– I'm what they commonly call fat, Geillis, the normal size for women now, really. My breasts hang too low, and I've hair on my stomach, and my right eye falls slightly at the top when I laugh – it's like a blanket that's been left in wrinkles on a bed, you know. Under it is a grey eye with hints of orange around the iris – all the women in our family are named after flowers. That's the only thing we kept, our names: we've never managed to settle anywhere.

— How come you were without a place to stay and grow old?

— I lost it.

— Why?

— A man took it.

— Where's your ma?

— She's gone.

— A man took her too?

— Aye.

— How come you know so much, Iris?

— Smart women taught me.

— How'd they teach you?

— They wrote the stories they were not meant to, were published by others who broke rules to do so, they sang the songs they were not meant to sing, stole time to make paintings that left breadcrumbs for those of us who came after them, so we might follow them through the forest and try to get out the other side; they acted in films, on streets, in bars, or I just listened, cleaning loos alongside them, or sat next to a stranger who'd chat away: those are all women who taught me.

— Have you scars, Iris?

— Aye.

— From what?

— My own hand did a few. My thighs, wrists, forehead, skull, in my bones that have never stopped hurting for decades. The worst are inside my head where they took the only thing I should own – that's what I am trying to . . .

– Get back?

– Aye.

– They went inside your mind and took you . . . away from you?

– Excised!

I feel the grip of your hand squeezing mine back for the first time, and it makes me unable to breathe for a second, and no matter what else comes from this I am so grateful you ever spoke to me at all, Geillis.

– You had things happen to you as well?

– Aye, from a little girl up, a lot of times.

– I'm sorry, Iris.

– Don't be sorry, Geillis Duncan, don't be sorry for me. We are not here to talk about me – I put a call out to the ether for you!

– Are you sure about that, Iris?

You laugh, and you sound less like a girl then: you sound like a woman. In these last hours you have grown stronger, and I begin to realise I am weaker than you.

– How'd you mean?

– You think that it is just me – Geillis Duncan, about to be hanged from the gallows before strangers for their own entertainment and the King's gratification, the one who will meet her maker and leave this mortal plain in a matter of hours – who needs saved here?

– Aye.

– No, there is no saving me, Iris from the ether: we are here for you.

– What for?

– To help you go back.

– What if I don't want to?

– What else are you going to do?

Our hands relax and let go. It's freezing in here now. I don't know how to spark a fire from the ether. Still, I can try.

– Will you do something for me, Iris?

– Aye.

– At noon on the fourth of December every year, will you come to Castlehill and bring me a rose? Will you lay it down and say, This is a rose for Geillis Duncan, who held my hand and made me smile and left this world long before me and was my friend a long, long time ago?

– Aye, I will.

– A rose – grey as the whisper of a tornado?

– What other!

Up on the High Street. How cobbles are laid like the skulls of newborns. They go all the way from castle to palace. A whole mile of them in neat rows. I am startled as the guard gets up in the corridor behind me. We can hear him cursing. He is over at the door, then the well, and seeing his boots. Clanking them up. We hear him hauling them on. I freeze. Geillis does not. He shuffles away outside. He'll be pissing in the Close. In a few hours' time fishermen will leave for Newhaven harbour – now as they

did then. Seagulls will wail, and the seals will fall – fat pups
with big beautiful black eyes – into the North Sea.

– What do you need, Geillis, whilst the guard is away?

– Just keep telling me stories.

– Once upon a time there was a world, and it was hung
up to spin in a universe without explanation. It was so
stunning. Outer space curled around it in black so it would
better shine. Stars travelled to gaze upon it from all
different parts of the galaxy. Many of those stars died
hundreds of thousands of years before. Light is a
time-traveller. All things are possible. One day many years
after the dinosaurs had gone and the fires had cooled and
set to stone and the ice had carved her valleys and melted
into great vast lakes, there was a first girl and she was born
from nothing – a pearl in the sea – atoms – particles.

– A first girl?

– Aye, and she was born with a secret.

– What?

– That she was made of the purest kind of magic.

– I bet she was too, Iris.

– The first girl was born knowing that the tide comes
in only to go back out, and she knew that time is only what
we travel. She knew her body was just a temporary, and
imperfect, dwelling for her own transient soul.

We hear the guard clatter along the dim corridor; he
lurches at the cell door, reaches for his keys.

I hold my breath – stand between him and you.

— Do you want to know something, Iris?

— What?

— You have feathers sprouting out of your shoulders.

— I don't!

— You do: I could feel them when we were out there floating in the Null.

— Angel feathers?

— No! You are no angel, Iris, you're a crow.

— I'm not!

— You are, my familiar. I knew you'd come to help me. Feel them piercing your skin — the barbs in the end of the feathers are like fish hooks, feel them . . .

I do then, puncturing through flesh, erupting so there is a tiny red raised mark around each feather as it buds, small on my neck, bigger on my shoulders, on my cheeks — fine black feathers begin to shine in the dim, and you are looking at me, Geillis Duncan, like you knew this was going to happen, but I never did, and I am scared, and the Null feels far from me now, and you are turning to hold your hands out to the pale light, not wanting to see the fear in my eyes as I turn. You sit down slowly and smooth out your skirts. I unfold my wings, and they brush against the guard's skin, and it gives him the creeps. Pockmarks rise with hair all along his arm, and he reaches for a bottle and hacks up a big phlegmy gob of spit.

— Who are you talking to, witch? Answer me, Geillis Duncan.

— I am not talking to anybody.

— Were there other guards in here messing around with my boots?

— Aye.

— You have a matter of hours left, hen — you're lucky I don't know when they are coming back, or I'd be in there to sort you out one last time.

He shrugs like he can't feel my feathers all over his face. Like his heart is not beating hard. Like he isn't walking away with jelly legs. Feathers pierce through my thighs; my ankles are black and glossy with feathers that are all fluttering; each toe has become a long, long claw — I am a crow, tall enough to stride around this little corridor looking at Geillis, who leans back against the wall, turns to me with a smile.

7

Geillis Duncan

5 a.m.
Memories (so they say):
1st August 2021 — cell on High Street, 4th December 1591
Elements: Water + Luna

If a pregnant woman looks at the full moon her baby will go insane. So they say. My grandmother told it to me. Her grandmother told it to her. I learnt to cross myself when the dead were taken by for a burial before I knew how to clean the grate. I learnt to bow my head to everyone I worked for, and rich women too – they always scared me with their thin faces and how they looked at me. I would dip my head low so they didn't think I was sharp-eyed. I let them know in all my actions that I understood I was less than even the lowliest of them. I talked softly to everyone at all times. Sharp tongues get women killed. That's what I was told. There is still a moon hanging up outside this cell. Iris checked for me before she left to drift in the place beyond here with her feathers and her little reptilian ankles. It's good she told me. They won't take the moon away. The sun will be here soon. It will be a white sky with a white sun that casts a cool glow rather than warmth. I can tell that without even going out there. I am going to miss my work. Isn't that silly? I liked to tend to chores for Mr Seaton. It was a good job. Not that I can think of him without bile burning my throat. How could he seem so nice to everyone and hate me so completely? In a matter of hours my voice won't exist any more, nor my hair being tugged by a breeze, nor my limp as I go to church. I won't ever see my family or friends or the sunlight making the fields in East Lothian blaze. I won't pluck and roast a chicken. I won't gut a fish or peel potatoes. I will not wake early to worry before the start of day. I blew away the drawings we scratched in the dust so the guard won't see them. After all they have done, I want to die now. There is no getting over what those men took from me. Not now or ever, and the only way my family will be okay is if I am gone. I have memories to give away before I meet God – so you can have them, Iris from the ether. Are you listening? Nobody else will write them down. It is you who has come to hear me. All the way down the corridor are three pronged footsteps in the dust.

You'll be back. I hope. My bones are splinters. It hurts to breathe. My lungs are full of water and dust. My ribs are bruised purple. My fingertips! Outside it might be snowing. That's a thing to think about, is it not, in the last hours of being alive? Light, tiny flakes of softest snow. What did Iris say? That I don't need sticks or twigs to fly from this cell? It's so much easier when I have her voice to soothe me. She has a way to dream out loud so I can see it – I don't think like she does. Going outside to die. That's what it will be. I haven't been free to walk outside for ever so long, and I wish I could just walk away from the guards and the King's men and the hangman, just go to the baker and buy a warm roll and take it back to my sisters and eat it and hug her wee fat baby and drink tea and listen to her talk about nothing. The baby will never know me now. No family is allowed to see me here. I wonder if they'll come to watch? I hope they don't. It is so cold in here. My breath is a mist. It unfurls in the air. Out of it sail two hundred witches, in sieves, in cauldrons, in wee paper boats, in buckets, in soup-pots, they are out there – what a sight it is to see! They are paddling out on the bay in North Berwick. It could be sieves, or it could be cauldrons. Look – the Devil is waiting! He wants his arse kissed. So they say. Each witch has to crawl on hands and knees to do so, or walk backwards. They call it the *osculum infame*: a kiss of shame. Witches all over the bay. So they say. Broiling up a storm so wild that the King and Queen could not even get close, but the witches I can see in my mind are all out on the sea in pure joy, not bothering anyone — they just leap up through the air, happy as porpoises migrating home. I think Iris has taught me how to dream.

Still, I will die today.

I will.

I will die.

Today, I will die, so they say.

Doctor John Fian, Agnes Sampson, Barbara Napier, Euphame MacCalzean — they are the ones I told on first, then they told on others, and now we are hundreds, and then we will be thousands and one day millions. It is a plague. A thought plague. How many people in this world will be killed by thought plagues? Those infections spread. They create nothing but fear and death. They take ordinary people to an early grave, or just scare them as they try to live out their days. Aye! A witch-pricker's finger can be pointed at any one of us. It chose me. There is a hangman's noose. There are cells and locked doors. We all know it. They belong to the people who own all of us. It's true the witch-pricker picked us out one by one, but he did not point with his finger. It is a chicken bone (boiled clean) that pokes out from his shirt-sleeves.

Look close.

You'll see it!

In each of his eyes there is a reflection. A whole rack of torture instruments. He has the glazed expression of a man paid in gold to act on behalf of a king who claims he is acting as a direct representative of God. There are good women, and there are bad women. So say all the crows.

Where is she – Iris? Is she there pecking that guard's eyes out?

I know she would now for me.

Iris does not know what I really want from her before this is through . . .

I think about the things that Iris says, that every man is taught he is the closest representation of God on earth. Every man knows the more powerful he is, the closer he is to God, the person that made the universe, so they act with the faith of men who believe the Creator is behind them, or so they say. Who can argue with a man who has the backing of a being who made the cosmos? Iris says I can say whatever I want when they walk me through Edinburgh's streets. How do I do it? Wait until I am right before the crowd? Do I tell the authorities? Do I just keep saying it to anyone who will listen until they kick the stool from under my feet?

I feel oddly me today.

As if I have come into my fullness.

Maybe that's how we all leave in the end.

I will neither beg, nor plead – there will be no hysterics, I won't offer my body.

I've done all those things.

One of the men asked if I would give him my . . . eyes.

He smelled of alcohol, and he asked if I'd pluck my own eyes out and hand them over and go away a blind girl forever more, and to my shame, because I was in so much pain and they wouldn't stop, I said, Aye! The man laughed at that. Laughed and laughed. See if there was a devil, I'd have wed him just so he'd kill all the ones that hurt me — don't they think about that?

I'd have demanded fire and brimstone for my wedding gift.

Men want to kill — they do — and it just so happens this time they picked me.

Because of this here mark on my skin.

So they say. Because I left a house at night. My employer was in debt, so they say. He got paid by the hour to torture me, so they say. Some kind of godly service to protect a King and his wife and all of mankind — against me.

So they say.

He is a godly King, and he says it all the time.

I had to play the Jew's harp — with my twisted broken fingers, for him.

He wanted to see how I played it for the Devil . . . He saw no irony at all in me playing it for him after what he had ordered done to me.

Who is the Devil?

Where does he really exist?

In the mouths and fists of men that lie as husbands and fathers and owners of this life!

I have memories to get rid of, I have memories to give away!

You must take them for me, Iris . . .

We had blue skies that morning.

First came the women walking down the High Street.

Upright and biblical – that's the kind of look they go for.

I swear their veins are twisted.

Those women were certain of their ability to see a sign.

All they wanted was to see it and tell it to the nearest godly man through their skinny pursed lips. Their evidence is found, well, just by looking. I looked! I saw! Torture the bitch! Kill, kill, kill!

They saw what?

A way to start a death riot for a godly man's approval?

It would seem those people believe they have no wickedness, but do not be mistaken – the things that have come out their mouths! The very same mouths that sing hymns in church every Sunday. They make piety a hand gesture, a nod, a whisper, a written note – profitable as it is for their reputation. My employer was in the tavern that day, and he fought with a man who had a dog that'd nipped at his heel. I was out for chores. Eyes were on me. Always! Iris says it's on account of my smooth skin and my straight back, but much more than that, they look at me because of how I shine.

I've tried not to!

Nobody likes a shining thing.

I tried all I could to find ways to stop doing that, didn't I, because it attracts the absolute worst of them. Iris said the darkest is always drawn to the brightest — they search it out even in their sleep. In their waking it is there at the back of their mind as they wash their face and start their day; they have a third sense keening for it on the street, in church. They are always looking for that glint of pure light. The absolute absence of light wants its opposite. So it can consume it.

I had seen a fox in the garden early that morning, the same one that had fox cubs in the church graveyard last year, so I was happy. The women were looking. I wouldn't have argued with any of them. I was in a good mood, but on other days . . . maybe! Arguing isn't a virtue. Anger is not a virtue. Pride is not a virtue. Being happy at seeing a fox with her cubs is not a virtue. I wonder which of those women up early in the wee hours this morning with their Bibles come to see me hang so they can go home happy? I wanted to go to the sea that morning. Instead I had to settle with lifting my gaze to get a glimpse of it far away, and then I was down an alley for one chore and another and counting weather as I used to do when I was still able to see it. Rain, mizzle, sun, snow, thunder, storm, or that grey I describe as eternal. Eternal grey! This country seems like that most of the time. The dullest place on earth. Those women were on the High Street. They were standing there all prim and loud with their thoughts. *Lucky to get a job at all, that one. My husband looks at it because she draws him with her mind!* It wasn't my mind that drew them. It was not that part of my body. Little unspoken pacts they made. Then they started their rumours. They all ended with *so they say, so they say*. Each of those women filed into a tea-room. Sat there like the world was their maid. They ordered scalding tea that was never quite hot enough. Poured it into bald cups from a dangerous height. I went back to Seaton's house because it was time to sweep and clean and bend and scrub and clatter and wash and scour and cut and slice and boil and bake and mend and fix, and all the while he was eyeing my youthful plump like it was goose fat for the Sunday roast, just about ready to be served on Sunday in the name of our good Lord.

I did my bit.

Gave a very, very small smile.

Not enough to seem like I had ever been happy.

Kept my eyes down.

Curtsied!

My nails were very, very clean.

I have always been polite.

I'm not a stupid girl. I know to say yes when I am asked to do a thing, only yes and thank you and of course and I'd be glad to and please allow me! I'm sorry. I say I'm sorry. I turn sideways in a hallway to let someone pass and press myself flat so they can get enough room to ride a bloody horse past and I say I am sorry. I must be sorry, therefore I am. Those were my allocated words, given at birth, pinned on my crib so I'd know. Since I learnt them, I just rotate them. I don't do that inside my head, though, not with Iris! I polished his silver. I swept the grate. I bought vegetables, making sure to pick the best ones. I gutted the fish. I threw fish scales into the bin and bones into the stockpot. I seasoned them liberally, just how he likes it. I wasted nothing. I mended his shirt. Darned his socks. I made his bed. Fresh sheets. Blankets turned down just right. I never let a complaint come from my mouth. Not on my birthday, or when my grandmother died and I couldn't go to her – even when she would only ask for me, saying my name again and again like she already knew what was coming, even then. I did not say a word that I was not allowed to nor did I ever ask a question of anyone. That would have been wrong.

Things were calling me.

Night, the moon, the sea – all called me and in that order.

I would have settled for a river.

Or a picnic in a meadow, or even a garden, just so I could be outside a while.

The stars wanted to snag at my hair, tug on it gently.

The moon wanted to pull me away.

The sea was calling for me like my grandmother had before she was gone.

The brightness of the stars!

I needed them, so I did just the one thing. And it is really this they are killing me for.

I went out at night.

Alone.

I got a lift (shouldn't have) and went to look at a big white rock out on the sea. Gannets dive on it all day and night. The Bass Rock turns pink when the sun goes down, and it is so pretty it's hard to believe it is really a prison. I found a shell. Flat and silver. I took it home and shined it in secret at night. I used the rough of my skirts to smooth down those ridges – then the oil from my finger to buff up the sheen.

It was like carrying around a secret moon.

8

Geillis Duncan

5.33 a.m.

Memories (Iris come back / the river flows):
1st August 2021 — cell on High Street, 4th December 1591
Elements: Water + Luna

Whenever I missed my grandmother I took the moon out and looked at it. I rubbed it when I went to sleep every night. Persuaded myself this one act, if repeated enough times, would keep me safe. On the next market day those women walked the streets as they did. All bone and marrow, red-veined, all tooth and claw, opening and closing their beaked faces and their tongues darting out all forked. I kept the shell hidden in my skirt pockets. Touched it when they made me feel scared to be seen by others. My own Luna shell to give me light when

I was afraid to show mine – it would reflect its own back at me. It made me so happy. One day I decided to bathe in his tin bath (as if I had the right), and my master stole it. Seaton! He took it. The thing I had that shined. There was nothing I could do. I didn't even say a word. I just tried even harder to cook his tea exactly how he liked, polished the silver twice, took his boots off for him at the door. Kept turning down the bed just perfectly with the triangle shape he insisted upon and all his shirts twice pressed. I did all of my duties better than I had before. He disliked me even more then. He muttered in other rooms where he knew I would hear him but not loud enough for me to say anything – as if I'd ever have had the courage or idiocy to do so. People would visit, and he would tell them I was doing things that I was not doing. He tried out different stories on varying audiences, to see how they'd react, to gauge what they'd say – to see if he could make them believe him. He didn't say it in public. Not at first. He told these stories, embellished a little each time, always in private to see if they had the right impact on the listener. He tried it with the butcher and the baker and the vicar and the scribe. That went well, so he said it to the lawmaker and then almost daily to his prize red hen. He was rehearsing, finessing the kind of story that could end in a teenage girl's death. He began to tell me I was dishonest and mistrustful and lazy. Over time, he taught me to no longer trust what I thought, or said, or even the things that my gut told me.

When I walked down a street, people began to straighten their spines when they saw me, as if I might take an inch from their height just by being near them.

Geillis Duncan is cursed with an ability to cure the ill.

So they say.

They said it in a whisper so I wouldn't hear, and then a cold wind blew down the lanes of North Berwick and all along the High Street, all the way across the fields – right up to my employer's door in Tranent.

Huff and puff.

Blow this door down.

Knock, knock, knock – can we see the bailiff?

We heard he had a story to tell?

Payment in gold for such stories, isn't there?

– Iris, I'm lonely, I'm scared. Please come back to me.

I think of Seaton and feel such disgust that any human could be built that way. I cry about it, but only on Sundays. Despite what he has done, I don't wish him dead. I will not take the mark of his evil on my soul. I will not let him make me the way he is: that kind of malevolence belongs to him, and I return it to him threefold – he will not spoil me bitter like the cream. There is mostly just good in me. His toxic bile does not belong in my throat to make my gut acidic and corrode my body as well as mind and soul. I am a healer. I was born like this. I am a pure one. I cannot choose to live, but I can decide to leave this world with men's hatred as the strongest mark on me. I am walking out of this cell in a few hours, and I will hold my head up and take with me the one thing people like him envy and seek to destroy or tarnish or dull or steal. Light. My goodness, my heart, my ability to heal. That doesn't make me a witch. Just as his poverty and debt and disease and desire to destroy all that is good do not make him an agent of God. Still, I sit here convicted, and he sleeps with a pot of gold. His name is David Seaton. I say it in my prayers to God over and over when I choose to believe – I try to pray to God, for my grandmother, once a week, like I know she would have wanted me to. His name is Seaton. It is your call, God. His name is Seaton. A man who gets solid from torture. A light-stealer if ever there was one. Witch-hunter. A man made almost entirely of hate. Why did I have to work for him? Of all the men who would have had me as a servant. I worked for one who walked these streets like they had been paved for him, especially after what he did to me. He started to tell the stories of witches, and before each ended he had stoked a fire of fear, and it spread across the rooftops and under the doorways and blackened the windows and left soot behind my every step.

Geillis Duncan is amphibian.

A big fat toad. Or at least she knows how to extract their venom, because her father was a toad and her mother was a half-toad and her grandmother was a snake. It was early one Friday morning when I saw her turn into a goat. She chewed up the neighbours' laundry on the line, and then she brayed at children on their way to school and butted the milkman so he spilt his buckets of milk, and then she tried to mount him, and she lost the man a day's wage. We all know about the girl Geillis Duncan!

My name was always on the tip of their tales with not one single thing true, but what glee they took in them. What a thrill to make me small, to make me wanton.

Can't get enough of men, that one — everyone's husband has had her.

All that, and the only sins I lay with were the ones they put upon me. My whole life no man had ever touched me until they came to bruise my skin and break body and mind.

Geillis Duncan sailed to Denmark in a sieve.

Geillis Duncan sleeps in the trunk of an old oak tree.

Geillis Duncan has a broomstick.

Geillis Duncan hates men.

Geillis Duncan is ugly.

Geillis Duncan spat at my child.

Geillis Duncan cursed the pavement so it's like walking on waves.

Geillis Duncan is strange.

Geillis Duncan is crazy.

Geillis Duncan drinks all the time — she does not even know her own mind.

Geillis Duncan met the Devil and begged him to take her to bed.

They said so many things.

I almost wanted to believe them. When you are so worn out, it becomes easier not to question anything they say. I was scared for my family. I was scared for my friends. I was scared for anyone who had shown me kindness. I was scared for anyone who wanted to stand up for me. Who would they point a finger at next? There was so much fear. I wanted so desperately for them to take away all their accusations and evil and madness and barbed words. There comes a point in torture where you will do anything. If they'd told me to kill, I would have. If they had said that I must go to the church and scream out loud that God was a damn flea I would have gone even further and said it to his face, and I would have stood on him and ground him into dust and shat on him and cursed the world and all who ever walked it — I'd have done it and then danced naked for them on hot coals.

They tortured me in the room that David Seaton had asked me to clean extra thoroughly that morning.

I did it unaware that this was preparation for their celebration.

I'd plucked a single flower and placed it in a tiny green bottle on the mantelpiece, and when they were torturing me I tried to keep my eyes fixed on it.

So much fun to lay into a girl, right?

Exciting for them.

It made them hard.

Take her down ten or twenty inches, make her grovel, make her bleed.

All rules were gone – it was their little party, and such power! In their eyes. In their fingers. Their thumbs. Their boots. They could do anything they wanted to me.

So they did.

– Geillis?

– Iris!

– I don't know how to talk quite right with this beak yet.

– You sound just like you. I'm dizzy with happiness to hear your voice again!

– We must be quiet!

– Why, Iris, do you think they might say I've been conversing with a crow and accuse me of being . . . a witch?

We both look towards the guard and are helpless then, laughter like peals of church bells on a morning when a baby is christened or when a bride bursting with love walks down the aisle, or when a sword is picked up – to slay a murderous bastard so his victim's family can sleep just a tiny wee bit better.

– Where did you go, Iris?

– I went to see the hangman. He's ready, he's on his way. Geillis?

– Aye?

– Do you really think it was you who put a call out to me in the ether?

– Aye, Iris, I do! Sorry about that. You're not going to set the witch-pricker on me, are you? You're not against me like those women were?

– Of course I'm not, calm down. I'm not, I promise, and aye, they'd think I was your familiar, all of them, and I'm beginning to think so too – see the spread of these wings . . .

– Impressive!

– Isn't it? This time in the Null I did put a call out, though.

– For what?

– You'll see.

– You know what, Iris, I always felt I had a best friend out there somewhere.

– The kind that would turn into a crow for you?

– Aye!

– Well, at your service, my lady.

A beautiful black-feathered wing spans out like an actor's cloak.

– Nobody has ever made me feel as happy as you do, Iris.

– Don't make me cry, Geillis; crows don't cry, everybody knows it. Did you know crows never forget a face? They can escort you over to the other side.

– Can you?

– Maybe.

– What if you sprout back into human form, but inside my cell? Naked!

— You better hope not — they'll think you've conjured another witch from the dead. You know, before I arrived here, when my body wasn't so faint, I had a witch's mark on my back, large and red. When doctors try to take my blood, they can never get it out my veins — and as for my pulse, it is so faint they often can't feel it all. No, no, I'm not dead! Don't look at me like that! I don't think I am, anyway, not at all. Shit! Do you hear those footsteps? That's the guard going out to talk to the hangman. The sun doesn't want to come and see this: it's a tiny wee bright moon still out there this morning, Geillis, and word is in the ether that you made me out of clay? Did you? Was my life a dream? Maybe you did. Maybe the earth made us all out of clay. Big witch that she is, biggest and baddest and best witch of them all! What else do they say? When a witch touches a dead body it may bleed. These were all things that James VI wrote in his book *Daemonologie*, the witch-pricker's bible; he's just putting down the notes in your time, Geillis, but he'll publish it before too long. They were crazy things that the King wrote. A witch will confess to having given her soul to the Devil. If a human dies without reason a witch shall be the cause. Supernatural strength equals witch. If they see an apparition (let's be quiet as ash, Geillis, I'm going to whisper) they are a witch, and that would make me feel bad if I were not just a time-travelling fact of life — not a familiar or a ghost; at least, I didn't think I was, anyway, but now I'm a crow, you've really got me thinking.

Turn my head and glint to her with tired eyes.

– Do you like it, Iris?

– Aye.

– Thought you might.

– Can you hear the footsteps?

– Aye. Tell me more, Iris, tell me things: slow time down, keep them away.

– The difference between conjurers and witches is that the first will make the Devil tremble in fear to do their bidding, whereas witches are more like, hey ho, it's all okay an that, let's just have a wee cup of tea, let's sit down, it's all civilised. Satan, d'ye like Earl Grey? Wee bit of lemon? Honey? An almond slice? No? Go on, have a slice! A conjurer can compel the Devil to do things, but a witch has to offer her blood or soul. (Why do we always get the lesser deal?) The conjurer acts from curiosity, but the broomstick brigade, apparently, behaves solely from malice. MALICE! Enchanters are not common. As for soothsayers or wizards, well, there's a bit of flying, and they fancy themselves as able to sing a song! Yes, they do, regular born crooners the soothsayers, rappers of the occult busting out rhymes. They can project images too, into glasses and stuff like that. Necromancers raise the dead to tell us secrets of future events. Perhaps that's what you are, Geillis? Am I the dead? I'm not sure you want to know much more than this, really. They're on their way – can you hear them?

— Just keep talking, Iris!

— Pythonissae specialise in artificial charms. Venefici deal with poison. It's all the same and back to the moon. It's always back to the moon. Witches will pull it down towards them. It's a problem. It could happen any time. The whole universe will tilt, and then we'll all be walking sideways. Sometimes a witch shows herself by hating someone she formerly claimed to love. It's proof, dear God, is it not proof? It is. None other needed. She will not stay steadfast in her faith. Weak for the Devil! Does she question man at all on anything? Witch! Consciousness is a river. All of us are linked.

— And they say there is no magic in this world?

— So, they say, Geillis.

— You are a river.

— I am a crow!

— You were a river first.

— Aye, you are getting it, my dear friend Geillis. Don't listen to them talking. They will be at this cell soon enough. You are a river. I am a river. Your consciousness flows to me. Mine to you. The ether is a tributary. We can travel through it. Back and forth. From where I am now to you — where you are, but more so, you can take all the tributaries that made up who you are and go back through them. Can you feel the sand under your bare feet as a child? You went into rockpools and caught tiny fish in your cold fist. Clear as ice you carved out the clouds above with fat little fingers long before you played a Jew's harp. Do you remember when your grandmother needed you . . . how you knew that you had to run home and open her door and pick her up from the hall where she fell? You did it, didn't you? You were barely seven years old. Your sharpness hadn't been dulled yet. Whilst you watched the women around you dim their light and wit at will, lest they be offensive to men (endangered, hunted, hanged, battered), yours was good until they tried to train it out of you as a girl. Still, you could look at a baby, and it knew everything about your soul. It giggled and gurgled and kicked its bare feet because it knew on sight that you are so, so good in heart and smart in thought, and when it saw your light it felt no fear or jealousy, only pure and complete joy!

Geillis, they still imagine the innate power of our nature can serve only him. Him! A hymn. Amen! They used a word to say what they did to you. Tortured. Eight letters. It is too little a word. I have never called directly to another like this across the ether, or maybe you did to me, or maybe we did to each other, but there are many seas and wars and decades and inventions and laws and deaths between us. So very many deaths have occurred from where you sit in your cell to where I sit tucked up in this nook so the guard won't see me. I will follow you on your last journey to the gallows.

— Iris?

— What?

— Thank you.

— Don't. It was me who needed you. I do know some things. I know what it is like to be locked in. I know how it is to have a group brought in to watch my rape. I was twelve for that one. I'm not a tourist, Geillis. I'm not a visitor in a real person's life. I did not come here to see the crimes committed against you and feel better in my own bed. I am not here for entertainment. I won't let your blood and claim exemption for my own. That rape wasn't the last by a long way. There was no such thing even as that word, really, was there, for what happened to you? My abusers were idolised as heroes in their communities, whereas your perpetrators were sent by a king and idolised by entire countries as Men of God. Your torturers were not just protected by law, not just endorsed by law, but incited by law to act in service to the creator of all things! As if going after a woman like you was something God insisted upon. Tell me what kind of god wants any of this? I would like to reassure you that five hundred years from now the fine line of misogyny no longer elongates from uncomfortable to fatal, yet I cannot. It's a form of brainwashing, isn't it? When you dared look at those men around you, what did you see? They all thought they were right.

— In everything!

— At all times.

— What woman could question that? A dead one!

— No, Geillis, not even those ones are allowed to be right: not in this life, not in the next. You had as much right as your brother did to hold an opinion. From a child you were raised to hide your hurt lest it offend boys or men. No matter what they did to bestow it upon you, they could never be wrong. If you question your brother, even, who claims to love and respect you, how offended will he be that you think you have the right to do such a thing? How many times have boys' eyes (even the nicest ones) looked back at you, knowing with utter certainty that they are right and you are wrong? Because every stone laid since Adam watched Lilith leave Eden has been with the sole intent of him never being shamed by a woman again. Ever since the first of days, woman was told she was here solely to serve and obey, to bend and twist, to hide the sharp tip of her tongue. God help her if she is a mirror. If she reflects back at them what they are without even trying. It's the shining, Geillis. You still shine, baby girl, brave woman, hero who is teaching me how to grow a beak and thick feathers and claws. You do! They say there is no such thing as a witch and to put your hand in another woman's body and turn her child to take it literally back from death and bring it into life — is not something we learnt from women who went before and something some of us are far more skilled and knowing at doing.

— We learnt to tell our stories only when the men were gone.

– My dear, sweet, smart, funny Geillis Duncan, they will always be after us, it seems. Only this week I have seen a man who murdered a woman get five years only. Another who poured bleach in a woman's mouth and battered her with a baseball bat did not get a custodial sentence because she was not considered to be vulnerable.

I see your breath as a mist, Iris.

It hovers in the dim.

Out of it sails millions and billions of women in sieves – or it could be cauldrons – all across the bays in every country in the world!

Witches cause infertility, so they say.

Can curse a whole house to no children.

They are the reason a woman might lose her child to miscarriage.

Or why a man might have no ability to procreate.

Can't get it up? Has to be sinister – witch business.

The Devil does his worst bidding through witches, so they say.

More evil in witches than in any other living thing.

I will be hanged by late morning, so they say.

A big crowd coming, so they say.

I must walk to see the hangman on my own, so they say. None of my people are allowed near me, and even if they could they might become the next person to have a finger pointed at them – there's always a danger, so they say, so they say. I am not walking there on my own though, Iris. Even if you are the only crow I've ever been pals with, I know you won't let me go out there on my own. You came here to help me come to terms with the truth that I will die today.

— Will I go too?

— What, Iris?

— Is that why you called to me, Geillis?

— What are you trying to say?

— If a witch dies, her familiar goes too, don't they?

— Aye, they do, Iris, so they say.

9

Geillis Duncan

6 a.m.

After dream-torn sleep (via seance):
1st August 2021 — cell on High Street, 4th December 1591
Elements: Earth + Fire

I hear the priest before I see him. A long creak, the thud as a door closes behind him. Footsteps echo along the stone corridor. The scribble of his pencil as he signs himself in. Draws himself up to his full height, adjusting his cassock. He breathes loudly. Short, fast inhalations, with a touch of wheeze: his lungs are not good. I'd have given him herbs for that, and he'd have thanked me too. He blesses the hallway, he crosses the guard, and then he turns the corner down towards my cell. Earlier, the guard put the extra candles out so the priest can inspect me better. I stand in the middle of my cell. I have my hands folded neatly in front of me. Iris flies down and uses her beak to comb my hair for me. She smoothes it down with her wings, nestles slightly into my neck – the only warm thing to have been near me in eternity. As the priest steps up to the cell door, Iris hides in the corner where he can't see her. She has placed herself exactly where she can watch him. I know she'd like to pluck his eyes out. Drop them in the hangman's bucket. Let them scoop those out instead of my head.

– What say ye, Geillis Duncan!

– I want to report the men that made me lie under torture, about what they did and that they made me accuse others of being witches when they are not. Neither am I, and nor was Euphame or Agnes or Bessie, or Fian, or any of them. None of us met the Devil or plotted against anyone, let alone the King.

– Report them?

– Aye.

– To whom?

– You.

– Why me?

– Because you want my last confession. This is it. Before the eyes of God, I am telling you not one word of a lie – they tortured me mercilessly until I said whatever they wanted me to.

– These good, well-respected pillars of the community – fathers and husbands, merchants, supporters of the needy, these upstanding Christian men? That is what you want to offer in your confession?

— They made me tell lies.

— So says a demon's puppet.

— The women I accused are not witches, and neither am I! They made up lies and got me to tell them so they'd stop doing . . . what they were doing to me.

I hiss the last bit.

— Doing what, forcing you to tell the truth that you lay with the Devil?

— They made me fear for my sanity, my body and my life. I am innocent in all of this.

— Liars, were they? Is it a lie when they say witches bring harm to infants?

I can feel the flutter in Iris's wings as she turns herself around to face the wall and closes her eyes and steels herself to dig her claws into the dirt only. I feel tears well up despite myself at her loyalty and her belief in me. I no longer thought I had it in me to cry.

— Aye.

— Godless children are weak to the words of a devil or his agent, the witch.

— I am not a witch.

— Were you a godless child, Geillis Duncan?

— No.

— Are there marks of the Devil under that filthy dress? Are they all over your body?

– No!

Panic in my throat. Iris is up on the window behind me then so she can fly right into his face if he dares come in here and ask me to show him.

– Why is there a crow in here?

– I don't know.

– Did you know they never forget a face?

– I didn't.

– Is that bird looking at me, Geillis Duncan?

Iris tips her head on her side so he knows she is, then she flutters up so she is just outside the window, trying to still the beating of her heart, much as I am trying to hold onto the gallop of my own.

The hangman is behind the priest then, with his keys from the guard who has left.

Door clangs unlocked.

When they step into my cell I grow smaller as my neck is measured, my height. The rope will be short. It can take a long time to die.

– Will it snap? The old priest asks the hangman as if I am not even here.

– No, it's a strangulation, much slower.

– She'll lose consciousness.

– Aye, she will, at some point . . .

They check my boots as if I'll be wearing them when they burn my body later on in the day. I hope when they set me alight black butterflies fly up and out everywhere.

He makes me pick up one foot so he can grab it more easily. Then the other. He measures them both like I might have differently sized feet, and he scribbles something down. What does it matter? Do they think I have something hidden in my boots? A knife! A tiny little broomstick that I can make full size just with the power of my mighty mind? The hangman looks rested and well fed and happy. I hate him. It is hard to swallow his peace.

I do not want to die this way.

— You'll be brought up by noon, Geillis Duncan.

— Aye.

— There will be a chance to say a last word before the sack is placed over your head.

— Do they have to do that?

— Aye, can't give you a chance to set a last curse on anyone when you die, Geillis, so don't think about trying anything.

I stand there with my easily snappable wrists and my chapped lips and my cold body and my dizziness and my lack of sleep and my faintness and all the lies they have designed about how they are heroes, and about my victims.

A witch!

An immoral woman, a seducer of demons. Do they really believe a word of it?

The hangman says a last whispered word to the priest and leaves. I stand with the feeling of the hangman's cold hands on my neck. They will be the last human touch

I'll know when he places the rope around me. In a trance, the priest's fingers trace the Bible, as if he is reading Scripture by fingertip, and he kisses the cross.

— Give me your true last confession, Geillis Duncan.

— I helped birth babies. I brought them safe into the world, I didn't bring harm to them.

— Liar, all witches hurt children.

— I'm not a witch.

— You are a witch, and I'd not trust you with any child, especially one who has not been baptised. Your kind have been known to eat them. If a child is seen walking by a river with their parents, you can just by the power of the thoughts in your mind throw that child into the water so they drown in plain sight, can't you? Don't play innocent with me. You're not just a young girl, Geillis, you are an agent of the Devil. I know exactly what you witches do. Give me your true confession so you may find some grace for your mortal soul.

— I am not a witch.

— You are a dangerous witch, Geillis Duncan, and you are not the first I have dealt with. I know you could turn a horse mad just by blinking; you could travel by air to the judge who tried you were he not protected by Christ our Lord; you can bring forward the future so you know what is coming. You strike as lightning. You cause death or disfigurement or injury just by a throwaway thought. Any child you had would be given over by you to devils. No matter what you say, you would do all of those things, Geillis Duncan, and once they are done, they cannot be undone, even by a man of faith. I am trying to help save your immortal soul before you meet your Maker. Tell me the truth.

— I have told you the truth.

— You copulate with devils.

— I have never been touched by any man, except my torturers.

— We will bring justice down upon you this morning, Geillis. Do not delude yourself: no angel will take you. The stars can only be moved by spirit, and you are called to pay for your actions and not ascend. You would only be able to fly out of here on a broomstick you had anointed with unguent made from the limbs of the unbaptised babies you killed — do you think I don't know all the witches' secrets? Other than that, the only thing that could save you would be the Devil's power, and he has left you, Geillis: he has left you to your fate, and he won't return. He has had his way with you, and you are useless to him now. You are left on this earth, and he cares not if you are burned, or hanged, or stabbed with a stake. Tell me, when he lay with you, did he use the semen of a human man?

— I have not lain with the Devil.

— Liar! Incubi and succubi have been uncontrollably drawn towards each other for all of time. Witches of bygone times had to be forced into such copulation, but it seems your generation agrees, willingly. You, Geillis Duncan will have participated in the foulest of servitude, possibly even from your twelfth year, and you abandoned all faith to do so!

– Sir, I am fifteen years old now, and I swear to you I would not do any of those things you speak of! I want to take back the accusations towards the other women . . . it is all I can do now to tell you the actual truth – which is that I lied. I want you to hear the truth before I go to be judged before God.

Iris has crept onto the ground between us. She has something shiny and silver in her beak, like a coin. She places it by my foot, and I stand on it quickly. She has brought me back my little moon. I can finger it in my pocket when they walk me out into the cold street and feel the eyes of every spectator on me. She perches up on the furthest right side of my cell so that she is above him, but he can't see her any more.

Don't pluck his eyes out, Iris.

Don't do it!

– I will ask you for the last time, Geillis Duncan: what do you have to say?

– I am cold, I am tired, I am frightened. None of this is because I lay with any devil. There is no fallen angel to give credit for any of this. There is just hunger and pain and the sad realisation that my life will not end with a husband, or grandchildren, or even my own babies. There will be no home with a hearth that I can decorate with willow baskets and flowers, no doorstep to clean, no meals to cook, no clothes to mend. Instead there will just be an early and long dark descent into nothing. The nothing we all try to avoid. I did not think it would arrive so soon. I miss my family!

Proper tears now, but he has no sight for them.

He raises his Bible.

Takes out a glass phial.

Unstoppers it.

He casts holy water in a rhythmic motion through the bars so it lands upon my skin.

I wonder how much he gets paid for this.

He is not listening.

My heart will not slow now until I die. Another new guard has taken over out there. Everyone seems excited. The priest has spittle around his mouth. He is brown-toothed. The spittle flays off into the air. His black gown hangs off skinny wrists as his bony hands meet in prayer.

How many witches will be brought to this cell?

And who will they be?

Just children, or girls, old or ugly, outcast, poor, strange, odd-voiced, limping or unholy or too tall or too pretty – who are we who walk this corridor, who sit in this cell, who listen to the stories, who say anything that is asked of us in the end? The delusions of others will lead to our final breaths. When will we, not as witches but simply as women, curse our accusers? Who else will walk out of

here to meet their death as I will? In a short while, I will
follow the priest, and he will go on to sleep tonight, glad,
as others will be, that they have killed me. As he prays and
rants and raves, a patchwork of human skin spans the
curved stone roof of my cell. It breathes. It is the skin of
all the women who will be in here. It is all colours. Tiny
hairs or dark ones or moles or red spots. Iris looks at me.
We watch in silence. It is all the human skin they have
flayed from women's bodies in different coarsenesses and
shades, and it is breathing. They have taken our skin.
Taken it from us all. And while some of us seem to truly
know it, others profit by making out they don't. They say
there is no such thing as a witch. I say there is no such thing
as a woman who holds power solely in service of a man –
devil or human – or God. I say I am a witch, but it is not
really what I believe. We are just women with power and
skills and an innate knowledge. That's what makes us scary.
Who are we? We are many. Then there are the stories the
King tells, and the guards, and the women encouraged to
spread them in gossip too, all the stories, all the time.
About those who bring a curse upon their neighbour or a
stranger in the street, who cause a sister-in-law's baby to
die in the womb. The King tells of women who can change
into animals or beasts and who know the future, who have
six different ways to cause harm to humanity; the King
tells of a powerful witch who caused abortions at will, and
how a princess had been told not to talk to her, not to

leave the castle, but she left and met the witch and found when her baby was born it was not in one piece but in separate bits: there was a hand, then a head, there was a foot, there was an arm, an elbow, a neck, a spine, and the reason this had happened was because her husband had incurred God's anger by not killing enough witches.

I do not know what to believe any more except that I caused no living thing to die, I took no will from man, I lay with no devil, but I have been at gatherings where some have tried; I have helped women be healed, and the elements are in me as much as they are there around us. However, I have not done what it is they have said, and neither have these other women; and the King has told most of these stories, along with the churches and the men on the corners and the women who have looked to serve their men, they've told those stories too and looked to see who they could use to prove their lies. Who I am going to call out this morning? I have a familiar for no reason I understand, unless she has come to take me to the other side. I needed someone to believe me.

The priest is taking the body of Christ again and holding it out to me.

— Geillis Duncan, I know you know about a woman who turned into a horse because she had not been ardent enough in doing holy things and had not confessed and had not taken the Eucharist and only when she did so could the minister — who could see her still as human although everyone else could not – return her to her former state as a girl. Do you know about the woman who has spoken of witches who collect male organs? Sometimes thirty or forty of them! A witch lays all those penises in the nest of a bird or puts them all in a wooden box. They move as if they were alive and eat oats or dried apples. A man who had lost his member went to a witch and asked for it back. She told him to climb an oak and to open a box she had placed there and pick out a penis, but he tried to take the biggest one he could find, and she had said he better not do it because that one belonged to the local priest.

– I do not know of any women like that.

The priest goes on: he is fevered, he does not hear me. He is lost. Chanting and caught up only in his own soul being saved. He drifts out the cell and up the corridor, still talking to himself and absorbed in his own journey. These are the kind of stories they've made up and used to hang women like me. This is the world of men where they are obsessed with how witches wish only to steal their cocks and hang them in the trees so birds will eat them. If I could believe me I would do so gladly.

– Geillis?

– Aye?

– When do I get to be human again?

– I don't know. You came to me as spirit and voice, and now you are crow. It becomes you.

– Life is so trying.

Who has heard a crow sigh?

I have, it's funny.

Iris comes to sit on my shoulder as I lie back on the ground, which is cold, and I feel my body for the last time, unseen — check those hip bones jutting out, stomach concave. I paddle my feet like I used to do in the sea. I turn my neck so Iris can tuck herself up under my cheek, and I rest my face on her soft feathers.

— Geillis?

— Aye?

— I love you.

— I love you too, Iris.

She spreads her wings over my eyes to give me some quiet hours in the dim. I have pulled all my hair over my face too, so it is as if there is no nose, no mouth, no eyes, as if the front of my head is the back and the back of my head is the other back.

10

Geillis Duncan

11.33 a.m.

In the final minutes:

1st August 2021 — cell on High Street, 4th December 1591

Elements: Frost + Light

Who will kill me? It should not matter. It shouldn't. Iris is gone. She will be back. I sent her to fly up to Castlehill to let me know if they've erected two sets of gallows. It will be me hanged by the neck in front of all until death, and it will be Bessie Thompson too. David Seaton is a vile man. A man who had no kindness for me, who envied my ability to feel. Who resented that I knew how to take a leech and draw poison from someone sick. Who saw the gratitude I got and felt bile towards it. Who watched me pick the right herbs to help a child's belly feel

better. Simple things, and no magic in them. I took the
ways he shamed me. Over and over, each day in small
ways and bigger ones, he sought to dull my skin and
weaken my heart (where the soul resides) so I would
better know my level of nothing. I thought that was all of
it. He was looking to bigger resentments, though. Ones he
could not hide, although he has to most folks, and his route
to get to her was through me. Euphame MacCalzean.
That's who he wanted. That's who he went after. This is
my true confession. He could not go after her directly,
being of nobility as she is and with money, and he could
not risk being accused of trying to hurt her. To kill her, in
fact. He could not have his motive – to try to get his hands
on her inheritance – as something that linked him to her
death. So what other way to put a woman to death? Have
her accused of witchcraft, that's what. What better time
than just as King James, the most God-serving of all
royalty, arrives back in Scotland looking for witches? My
name is Geillis Duncan, and I will be hanged until dead in
a matter of minutes because Mr Seaton my employer used
such violence against me that I accused the one person he
really wanted tried – Euphame, a woman who was so
powerful and rich that even her husband Patrick had taken
her last name. Who has heard of such a thing? Euphame
was already a wealthy heiress when her mother-in-law left
Patrick and her even more money. Almost none went to
Katherine, Patrick's sister. And Katherine was wed to

David Seaton. So who hated Euphame? Who wanted her money? Who thought his wife should have inherited it? Who did he want me to accuse? Who was the first person I named? David Seaton started the North Berwick witch trials to try to get Euphame's money. Everyone knows it! Even the King. The judge, the jury, the guards, the priest — I bet they all know too, but nobody is going to dare open their mouth except for me.

I will speak, and nobody will stop me now.

It is my decision.

They can't hang me twice.

I am not yet dead in heart and mind.

They have pushed me beyond all things.

Before I stand in front of God, I will tell the truth so I am not tried on arrival as a liar in the next world.

I feel so guilty.

David Seaton made me accuse Euphame MacCalzean of using magic to kill their mutual father-in-law so she would inherit his money. I had to say that Euphame held the Sabbath convention where I played the Jew's harp. There were so many things they did not like about Euphame, but that she had money and power and did not fear her husband was the worst of it. To add insult to injury, her three daughters were the ones who would inherit her fortune upon her death. Euphame had already gone to court to protect her lands from members of her own family. Her only male heir had died. There were vultures circling her estate and testing her power. I did not know Euphame, but I saw her stride through North Berwick sometimes. On the last day I saw her, huge dark grey moths trailed behind her skirts, and in their wake were clouds of dust, and in the haze were hundreds of women who would be hanged or burned alive – thousands in the end is what they say will come from this, and I am only a pawn in a nasty, cruel game, and I will pay for it with my life just like Euphame. I sat in my cell and cried and cried and cried on the day of her execution. I never knew her, but she died that day because of me.

Before I go, I will confess, because although I am done with the world of men, I desperately want God's forgiveness. The window darkens as Iris squeezes though it.

– You look a touch plumper and glossier, my dearest Iris, what have you been eating?

– I ate a rat. I found it rotting in a back street. Tasty.

– I see. Tell me, what is happening out there, my pretty crow?

– The hangman has set up at Castlehill.

– What's he doing?

– He's chatting and telling jokes with the men that built the gallows.

– Is there a crowd?

– Aye! Can't you hear them?

We listen quietly for a minute and right enough there is a hum and throng of people away up out there.

— Did you see Bessie?

— Aye.

— Could she see you?

— Aye, although she thinks me a dream sent directly from you. I told her what you are going to do, that you have told the truth and you will tell it again no matter whether or not they believe you.

— Will she do it as well?

— Aye, she's shouting it at anyone who comes near her: she's said that they tortured both of you so you'd accuse Euphame and Agnes, all of them.

— Do you know what I keep seeing when I close my eyes, Iris?

— What?

— Euphame.

— Doing what?

— Being burnt alive.

— I can't imagine.

— They burnt her with the wood they were going to use on Barbara Napier. Before they killed Euphame it was Agnes Sampson. I accused her too, said she was an elder witch, and they tortured her until she confessed then they garrotted her in the end, and burnt her at the stake.

— Horrific.

— It was on the twenty-eighth of January this year, and I've thought of it every day since. They say Agnes haunts Holyrood Palace now, and I hope she does. I hope nobody sleeps well in those big fancy beds for fear a witch will come and take them away on her broomstick when they are dreaming. I hope the men check their cocks are still there morning, noon and night.

— Geillis?

— Aye?

— It's almost time: what can I do for you?

— Other than turn yourself into a crow so you can see me through to the other side?

— Aye.

— Tell me what is going on outside.

— There's a clatter of wheels on the High Street.

— The luckenbooth men?

— Aye.

— What else, Iris?

— I can see the old guard outside: he has shined up his shoes and is trying to impress a woman. There are still lots of footsteps heading towards Castlehill — all of them are, I think.

— They're all coming to see me die?

— Aye.

The cell door is unlocked slyly.

I shudder.

This time the hangman stoops when he comes in — he has put heeled boots on.

— You will stand to be brought to your execution, Geillis Duncan!

His voice booms.

I try not to notice as Iris watches me scramble upright and looks sadder than anyone would think a crow could. Some new guards hold open the cell door. My arms are tied roughly and tightly behind me. I walk out. Down this corridor is a patchwork of human skin too, and it is breathing. I'd like to say I have it in me to hold my head high and not be frightened, but as they lead me out into the bright – brightest of light – tears stream down my face.

I shake so badly.

The men hold my arms up on either side to half drag me. I can barely walk. Noise and light assail me. I have been in the dark for months. The guards force me in front of them, and the crowd parts to let me through. There is a cacophony of voices and eyes upon me – people cross themselves as I pass, children too. Nobody will meet my eyes. Lest I curse them or they see the truth in me. I catch a glimpse of my cousin. She has her head bowed in a hooded cloak, trying to not show she is crying. She is wearing my grandmother's cloak. I strain my gaze over the crowd. They are all here. My family! Hidden all over the place, they are – my aunts, my cousins, my uncles, my mother too, even though she barely raised me. They have come to stand before the gallows. I will not die alone here today. I didn't want them to see this, but now we are here I am glad those who know me have come to stand in silence against what is going to be done. Swoon when I see the gallows. Hot liquid down my legs. Up above on the rooftops, Iris glides down to land on a spire behind the gallows – then another crow, and another, as if a great, great many witches are flying here today, to help my spirit cross to the other side.

11

Iris

Noon
Taking flight (no more seance):
1 August 2021 — gallows on High Street, 4th December 1591
Element: Darkness

I have never watched a teenage girl prepare herself to die before, one who has been starved and tortured and assaulted, one who knows they will kill her before a hungry crowd. And I don't think I could ever manage to do so again. Geillis is not going to be allowed the chance to die quietly, on her own, in her older years, with people there to hold her hand. It is noisy. Staged. Geillis looks utterly tiny as she steps up onto the platform next to the gallows. They have to lift her up under her armpits to place her head in the noose, the way her father would so she could pick apples off the trees as a child. The spectators are in more than their hundreds – there are thousands here today. The crowd snakes away down the closes and streets and behind us; all the windows are open and people are looking out and talking loudly, and some of them are drinking or chewing on food or laughing.

These people are taking entertainment in my friend Geillis Duncan so brutally losing her life. There was a knowledge in me before I did this, and it arrived as a pure dread. I knew that coming to Geillis meant I could not be passive. Too many other people live their lives like that. Silence is complicity. Non-action is a form of approval. I will not be passive.

The hangman checks the rope fits around Geillis's neck. He takes it off. Her legs go. He ignores that and tests the strength of the knot. I bet that rope is so rough on her skin. Geillis Duncan is pale and thin and bony from being so underfed. I don't know when she last felt sun on her skin. When she last lifted her face up to greet the sun's late-afternoon kiss. This day is dull. A haar has come down across the city. No light will touch her again. I am so full of rage, perched up here on a tiled roof looking down at all of them calling out, baying for her death. I can't control it any more, I place a hex on every witness who takes glee in this – may a plague arrive one day to cast down every last one, may it pursue their children, and their children's children. If your grandmother took pleasure in this, may you pay for her sins.

Hex!

My soul will be taken for doing this, but I don't care about that any more.

To bear witness means to risk your life.

Otherwise what is it worth for those who have to die?

We all come out of darkness.

Every last person who ever walked this earth.

That's where we were. Before all things! It was what we knew first. We were in the space before time. It held us formless and colourless and boneless and mindless. It was the time when we were most true.

To what begins, we must return.

All things live in a perpetual circle.

Growth and decay.

Light and dark.

A beginning is only concluded by the ending.

We all know the end is coming back towards us – from the very first light.

We see it up ahead.

Get glimpses of it.

A feeling when sat outside in a cafe on a busy street, after a hot day, watching people, feet tired, our happiness pierced by something that won't let us be. Death is the final point of it all. Leaving makes our arrival complete. You knew this long before me, my dearest friend, my brave, gentle, defiant, careful, funny Geillis Duncan. While I went to a bed in a house with lights, you sat upright in the darkness.

The crow can also be a stealer of souls. I don't want Geillis to die like this. I don't want her to be in her body when it happens. I did not realise I had come here for this. In the crowd there are women. Quiet. Stepped back. Not wanting attention brought upon themselves. They are here to send Geillis some of their light. How their love for her shines. In the darkness! Their love has such brilliance that, no matter who dulled their skin or taught them to cast down their eyes, it still shines.

There are hard-faced mothers here with their children. They want to show what happens if you ever lose your faith. The children's faces are ruddy with excitement. There is a sense of performance, a show, like when the King took a witch aside so they could talk for a while, cast himself and Agnes on a stage in that moment so the commoners could picture it, so they could know that this was the story, these the characters, this the good one and this the bad one; this one serves God, and the other the Devil, here is the outcome – this woman is a witch.

We are not just crows here today.

They call a flock of ravens an unkindness. See them landing?

Up there on the tenement roof.

Tucked into the eaves or nestled behind chimney-pots.

One little girl looks up and yanks at her mother, but she is told to be quiet. They say ravens mate for life. They remember those who have wronged them. They remember those who have gone against others too. It is painful not to sit on Geillis's shoulder as she steps up now onto the stool. It is too low. She is too short. A flurry of fingers point. Someone runs. Comes back with a small set of wooden ladders. They are placed below the rope. Geillis holds a tiny feather of mine in her hand. There is a shiny moon in her pocket. Her feet are bruised, her limbs pale: she looks like a child, lost and unfed and uncared for. Out of habit she curls her fingers up into her fist to hide the mangled tips.

The hangman stands tall.

He is wide-shouldered.

The noose is ready.

Geillis is to be hanged first. Bessie will follow after. I fly down to land in front of her, and all I can see on her face is an incredible sadness and dignity. I understand only now how very precious Geillis Duncan has become to me.

It was wrong of me to think I was anything other than her familiar.

The world I told her about is only a dream now.

She goes up the first wooden step with her hands bound and shouts to the crowd.

— My name is Geillis Duncan. I am no witch, and neither was Euphame MacCalzean or Agnes Sampson.

David Seaton made each of us lie – they tortured me until I said what he had told me to say – they were not witches, and nor am I!

Nobody is listening.

The hangman shoves her towards the steps, and she begins to climb them.

The crowd begins to roar louder.

I can still feel your bony body under my feathered shoulders.

What will become of you and me?

They have things to say about birds. A group of grackles is called a plague. We crows are a horde, we are a hover, we are a mob and a parcel, we are a storytelling, we are a parliament. We gather in the trees high above you humans so we can discuss what? Magpies in a flock are called a tribe or a tiding. Buzzards gathering are a wake. There is a confusion of chiffchaffs. A chattering of choughs. Cuckoos are an asylum. There is a prayer of godwits. A cast of merlins. A murmuration of starlings. A quilt of eiders. A wisdom of owls. A quarrel of sparrows. A scold of jays. A charm of goldfinches. A chime of wrens. A commotion of coots. A conspiracy of ravens. I watch as birds fly here from all over the country to rest on rooftops and lintels and chimneys and windows.

Witches.

Geillis climbs up the last wooden steps her bare feet will ever feel, and her toes grip as if they might save her –

those tiny toes her mother kissed. Her boots are long gone. Those wee hands first played songs for her grandmother and brought to her heart only a pure and utter joy. First she played a whistle, then a flute – music was just in her is what they said, even when she was a little girl. When a beat was tapped out on someone's knee she'd bend and stretch like dancing to music was the real thing she was born to do. Running her hands over herbs in the garden or flowers in the meadow as a girl, all the wild ones she liked best, picking them and pressing them and learning about them. Waking up so excited one birthday morning when she got a gift of a cake. Then one year, there it was – her true calling – a Jew's harp.

Your eyes shine even now in this last second, don't they, Geillis Duncan? Even from here. They have taken on a glow. My tail is the shape of black diamond. You reach the top step, and the hangman settles the noose around your neck, places a bag over your head and as soon as I see you are in darkness I lift off and soar towards you. The air is so cold now. Out of nowhere, snow, then hail, begins to pelt the uneasy crowd, and they call out. Glide close enough over their heads so they feel feathers, as if a ghost of the future has passed them.

– Before the King's court and God himself, Geillis Duncan will be hanged until dead.

Bays from the crowd.

Children jump up and down.

A man sways, drunk, leers around him at women in the crowd.

Many hold crosses up, or touch them to their lips, mutter prayers under their breaths.

Geillis rubs her leg with her foot.

— I didn't do it!

At first her voice sounds like it is in my mind.

The hangman raises his hand, but the legal clerks shake their heads lightly.

— I hurt nobody. They tortured me until I told . . . their . . . lies!

A tight look on the clerk's face.

They know.

She isn't what they say she is, and they all know it — the clerks, the hangman, the women, the kids — but they want to believe the people in charge know what they are doing, and if that noose was not tight around her neck, I think rather than hear the truth they would bite and kick and punch her to death.

As the hangman pulls back the wooden steps, she drops, swings out towards the crowd, back, noose tightening like a fist around her throat. Her oxygen levels fall. The noose presses on her arteries. Blood stops travelling to her brain; it presses on the trachea, and her pulse grows faint as her brain begins to swell, and her legs are kicking out, and she cannot see anything, but she can hear the crowd shout, and while she will lose consciousness in less than a minute, it will take more than twenty for her to actually die, so before her aunts and cousins and mother walk away from this crowd, their mouths in straight tight lines, before they arrive home and sink to their knees and cry and cry and cry, before tens of thousands, millions, more women are tried as witches, before the King ends his life as an incoherent slobberer, his tongue grown too big for his mouth, before his wife leaves him and throws a wedding dress in the sea that was handmade by three hundred tailors, before the moon lights ice all over these streets tomorrow morning, before the hangman says his last words and Geillis Duncan's body swings limp and her arms droop, before her body is left to hang in clear sight all day, before all of it, I realise that I'll never return to my world again. You don't converse with a witch unless you are willing to die. Before the ether comes to claim my friend Geillis Duncan, I fly in front of the hangman and hiss the word *hex*. I place a hex on every man, woman or child who takes pleasure in Geillis's death, and my own hex is to never return to the dream I once had of a future.

I will not leave here today with my life.

It's time to let go.

This was always going to be the way I would die.

A long, long time from now, a young woman will be found in a flat on Castlehill, opposite where the gallows used to stand, and there won't be any identifiable reason as to why she has lain there decomposing alone for so long, but all down her hallway will be hundreds of crow feathers, and here and now, more importantly, my dearest Geillis will not feel the last fade of consciousness, nor the final swing of her body as she glides up and out of the noose and right into my winged heart and form. We fly in front of the hangman's face and over the rooftops, as her human body swings slower far, far below us: we soar – together. We ascend higher and higher, away from Castlehill and her gently swinging corpse. Away too from mine. I've never felt a stronger beat to these wings.

THE END

A Grey Rose fir Geillis Duncan

It's a storm, and a needle
and a ship,

ragged sails,
choppy waves

tilting the tiller
to navigate

a strait smaller
than a steel eye –

North Sea spindrift,
colder than ice,

a cell and a feather,
a human crow –

Geillis Duncan
put a call out to the ether

for her familiar;
it's a seance

in the sixteenth century:
wouldn't have gone,

if I wasn't willing
to die there.

It's grown men —
God endorsed,

paid in gold
and infamy,

to torture
a teenage girl,

sentence her to death —
tell me whose sins

she shall die for exactly?
A short drop,

hanging is slow,
could take forty-five minutes

before her feet will still.
I have a grey rose,

like a tornado,
to lay on Castlehill.

Acknowledgements

In honour of the story of Geillis Duncan, a small offering.
With thanks to Jamie Crawford, Edward Crossan and everyone at Polygon.

In Darkland Tales, the best modern Scottish authors offer dramatic retellings of stories from the nation's history, myth and legend. These are landmark moments from the past, viewed through a modern lens and alive to modern sensibilities. Each Darkland Tale is sharp, provocative and darkly comic, mining that seam of sedition and psychological drama that has always featured in the best of Scottish literature.

Rizzio Denise Mina autumn 2021

Hex Jenni Fagan spring 2022

Nothing Left to Fear From Hell Alan Warner 2023